Christmas Angel Song

by Monica DiIorio

Illustrations by Kate Adams

Spork, An Imprint of Clear Fork Publishing

Christmas Angel Song

Summary: When Seraphina the jolly angel is remembering the first Christmas, her friend Dominic, the angel has an idea."I wasn't there, but every angel knows about the night the Son of God was born. Can we remember that holy night together?" Dominic asked.As Seraphina and Dominic recall the events of that holy night, Dominic is inspired to sing as a special way to remember and celebrate the night of Jesus' birth. As the two angels sing God's praises the sleepy pine grove comes alive around them. The woodland animals stir to add their own contribution to the celebration. Choirs of other angels come to join in song with their own stars to put on top of the lovely pine trees in the forest. In the end the sleepy pine forest is awake with the sound of the angels' singing. The most important aspect of the book is of course the brief retelling of the first Christmas. However, this book also has an encouraging message which helps children understand that they can celebrate and remember the first Christmas in meaningful ways as well.For more information about Christmas Angel Song, go to monicadiiorio.com

Clear Fork Publishing
P.O. Box 870 102 S. Swenson
Stamford, Texas 79553
(325)773-5550
www.clearforkpublishing.com

Printed and Bound in the
United States of America.
ISBN: 978-1-950169-81-8 (hardcover)

An Imprint
of Clear Fork
Publishing

For Paul, Kate, Lauren, Jen, Andrew, Logan, Mom, Dad and Aunt Betty with love. Thank you for your love and encouragement. For our God and Savior Jesus, the Blessed Mother Mary and Saint Joseph with love and gratitude. - M.D.

For my Grandparents, Phil and Marie DiIorio, who always supported and encouraged my artistic endeavors. Thank you, I love you always! - K. A.

One jolly angel flew over the sleepy pine forest, towards a beautiful church. There was a tall pine tree next to the church and the angel placed a shining star on the top of the tree.
Another angel watched from behind a pine tree.

The smaller angel flew out, "What are you doing, Seraphina?"

"Oh, hi Dominic," the angel laughed. "I'm putting this star on the pine tree to remember another night when there was a special star up in the sky."

"What do you mean?" Dominic wondered.

"I am talking about the night Jesus was born." Seraphina answered.

"I wasn't there, but every angel knows about the night the Son of God was born. Can we remember that holy night together?" Dominic asked.

"Of course." Seraphina began. "The Savior Jesus was born in Bethlehem a long time ago. Mary and Joseph traveled to Bethlehem from far away. There was no room for them at the inn, so they had to stay in a barn with animals. After he was born, the baby Jesus lay in a manger filled with straw. He looked so sweet and tiny. His face was shining with peace and love."

Mary, his mother, bent to kiss his face with happy tears shining in her gentle eyes. Joseph was caring for baby Jesus and his mother.

Everything was bathed in the golden light of the Christmas star.

"Shepherds came to the barn to see Jesus." Dominic said.
"Yes," Seraphina said. "They had been told about the birth of
the baby Jesus by angels."

"There were angels like us also at the barn that night." Dominic said.

"Yes," Seraphina said. "There were many of us there that night. I was part of the choir of singing angels. We sang of our love for Jesus from above the barn."

"I wish I had a special way to remember that first Christmas."
Dominic said as his wings sagged a little.
"Let's go inside the church," Seraphina suggested.
"Praying always makes me feel better."

They went inside the church and knelt before the golden tabernacle. Inside the tabernacle, Jesus was present in the Blessed Sacrament. Then the two angels prayed with their hearts filled with love for the hidden Jesus.

"Remember Dominic, God can see the love we have in our hearts when we do something to show our love for him. Whatever we do whether it is big or small the love that we do it with is what matters." Seraphina explained.

"I have an idea!" Dominic said. "My way of remembering could be to sing like you did that first Christmas! Let's start singing!"
Dominic quickly flew out of the church. Seraphina was right behind him.

Together among the pines they sang…

"We're filled with joy each day of the year,

Come angels please join us and sing here,

Glory to God in the highest and

peace to his people on Earth,

Our loving, forgiving Jesus,

we sing of the night of your birth…"

As they sang, squirrels and racoons played beneath the trees. Rabbits and deer were leaping in time to the music. Brightly colored birds flew from Heaven to hang streamers of sweet-smelling flowers on the trees. Each of the birds sat on the snowy branches like tiny, colorful decorations.

Dancing angels held hands and whirled in merry circles around the trees.

Others played colorful wooden drums, long silver flutes or rang small golden bells.

Choirs of angels came and filled
the night sky. They carried their
own golden stars. They swirled
through the air and danced
among the falling snowflakes.

The swirling singing angels added their own stars to the tops of the other pine trees. Hundreds of stars now shone in the wintry night. The pine forest had become a place of giving glory to God and remembering the night Jesus was born.

Seraphina and Dominic laughed at the joyous place they were in. It had been a sleepy pine forest and now it was awake with the sound of the angels singing.

Children everywhere can join the angels in giving thanks to God for the special gift of the baby Jesus.

When children do good things and sing with love in their hearts for God, they too will be joining in the Christmas angel song.

Monica DiIorio is a wife, mother, grandmother and author. She loves living near the ocean in a tall yellow colonial in Connecticut. She has two cuddly cats who lounge on the furniture, blue hydrangea bushes in the yard and a teapot collection in the kitchen. She has spent many happy years working in education and in libraries. In particular, she has previously worked as a school librarian for elementary school, middle school and high school. Monica DiIorio is also the author of a humorous chapter book for grades 4-7, Baxter the Unusual Cat. It will be published in spring of 2023 by Clear Fork Publishing!
www.monicadiiorio.com

Kate Adams grew up near the coast of New England, where she enjoyed many days both in the woods and on the beach with her family. Those days helped cultivate her love of the ocean, nature and animals, which have inspired her to this day. She attended many art schools over the years and is disciplined in a wide variety of art forms, from traditional oil painting to graphic design. Throughout her career, her favorite subjects continue to be landscapes and animals, which she will recreate on the nearest medium available, whenever given the chance.

CPSIA information can be obtained
at www.ICGtesting.com
Printed in the USA
LVHW070129111022
730422LV00012B/549

9 781950 169818